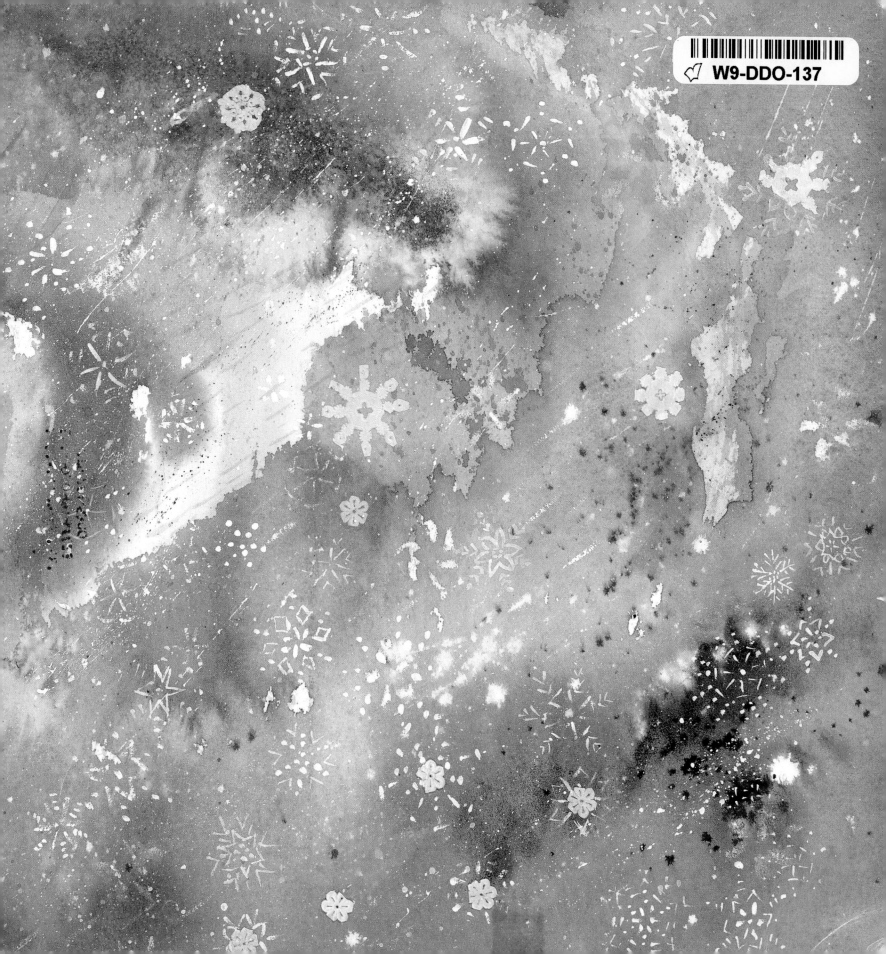

ELISA KLEVEN

SUN BREAD

DUTTON CHILDREN'S BOOKS ❀ NEW YORK

With love to Paul, Mia, and Ben

Special thanks to Scout and Jenny, our dear dogs, for modeling.

Copyright © 2001 by Elisa Kleven
All rights reserved.

CIP Data is available.

Published in the United States 2001 by Dutton Children's Books,
a division of Penguin Putnam Books for Young Readers
345 Hudson Street, New York, New York 10014
www.penguinputnam.com
Designed by Ellen M. Lucaire and Carolyn T. Fucile
Printed in Hong Kong
First Edition
ISBN 0-525-46674-6
1 3 5 7 9 10 8 6 4 2

The wind it whooshed, the snow it whirled,
The rain streamed down; it sloshed and swirled
And washed the colors from the world.

Bare trees shook like chilly bones.
Children grumbled in their homes.

Birds and beasts all wished the sun
Would show its golden face again.

A baker missed the sun so much,
She took some flour from her hutch,

Some butter, sugar, eggs, and yeast;
She said, "I'll bake a sunny feast.

Because the real sun likes to hide,
I'll make my own small sun inside."

She kneaded bread dough, rich and gold,
Glossy, springy, smooth to hold.

She shaped a bread so round and grand . . .

It seemed the sun shone in her hands!

Perhaps the baker's loving touch
Helped her sun bread grow so much.

Perhaps it was the yeast or flour—
Something gave that sun bread power!
It rose and rose and rose and rose. . . .

A smell from heaven filled the nose
Of every chilly child and dog,
Every porcupine and hog.

They saw that good bread rise and shine
And stopped their grumbles, groans, and whines.

"The baker's made a sun!" they cried.
The baker let them all inside . . .

And filled them up from toe to head
With puffy, hot, delicious bread.

Bread so brilliant, bright, and sunny,
Summer seemed to fill their tummies.
Bread so fluffy and so fine,
They felt themselves begin to shine . . .

And then—surprise!—begin to rise,
To float and flutter, flip and fly,
Light as kites, into the sky . . .

And down again, to dance and sing.
They all joined hands and hooves and wings
And praised the joy good bread can bring.
They made a sound so sweet and deep . . .

The real sun woke up from its sleep!
It burst out through the lumpy clouds

And streamed down on the startled crowd.
"The sun is here!" They gave a cheer.

"It wants some bread," the baker said.

So everyone threw bits of bread,
Chunks and hunks and crusty crumbs,
Into the sky, up to the sun,

Who ate it up and beamed back down
On every city, field, and town.

It dried the fur of mouse and dog
And warmed the soul of bear and frog.

It glittered on the blue-green seas,
Wove golden ribbons through the trees.

It painted colors on the day,
Melted all the snow away,
And brought the shadows out to play.

It scattered rainbows, soft and bright,
Fed the plants with its clear light . . .

WHEAT

Streaked the sky red, yellow, pink,
And purple—then began to sink.

And as the sun slipped down to rest,
The baker shouted this request:

"Come back for breakfast, please, dear sun.
I'll bake fresh sun bread—and sun buns!"

The baker baked the whole night long . . .

FIESTA BAKERY

Breads, Cakes
custom-made
for any size
appetite

And then—hooray!—at crack of dawn,

The sun was back to spread its light
Like honey on each yummy bite . . .

And dance around the world and sing
Of all the joy good bread can bring.

And now, when it is cold and gray
And dark and icy, guess who plays
With flour, sugar, eggs, and yeast?

Guess who bakes bread stars and beasts,
Bread birds and flowers, boats and towers,
Tons of buttery, small suns,
Which shine until the real one comes?

The baker and her crew—that's who!